CYRUS
THE
UNSINKABLE
SEA SERPENT

BILL PEET

HOUGHTON MIFFLIN COMPANY BOSTON

A sea serpent for T. J.

For information about permission to reproduce selections from this book,
write to trade.permissions@hmhco.com or to Permissions,
Houghton Mifflin Harcourt Publishing Company,
3 Park Avenue, 19th Floor, New York, New York 10016.

Printed in China
ISBN: 978-0-395-20272-2 REINFORCED EDITION
ISBN: 978-0-395-31389-3 SANDPIPER PAPERBOUND EDITION

SCP   55 54 53 52 51 50 49 48
4500823083

Once upon a time there was a giant sea serpent named Cyrus. Even though he was a horrible looking monster he wasn't the least bit fierce. All he ever did was wander about in the sea with no idea of where he was going.

"I'm tired of wandering," said Cyrus one day. "I wish there was something more exciting to do. I'd like to have some fun for a change."

"If you want to have some fun," said a shark, "why don't you go out and wreck a ship, then eat all the passengers?"

"Oh no," said Cyrus, "I couldn't do an awful thing like that. Besides, I never eat people, I only eat sardines."

"You've got no more spunk than a jelly fish," sneered the shark. "You're nothing but a big sissy."

Cyrus had never been called a sissy and it made him furious.

"I can be as rough and tough as anyone," he grumbled, "and if I have to wreck a ship to prove it, that's what I'll do. It might even be fun."

The serpent raised his head high out of the water to search for a ship, but as far as he could see there wasn't a sail.

"I know where I can find ships," he said, "lots of them."

He went cruising along the seacoast until he came to a harbor, and there sure enough were ships by the dozen riding at anchor on the quiet water.

"I'll just lie low," Cyrus decided. "Sooner or later one of them will head out to sea. Then I'll have some fun."

After a quick look around to make sure no one had seen him, the serpent slipped under a pier to hide in the pilings.

Pretty soon there was a great commotion and a confusion of shouting voices as a crowd poured onto the pier. A ship was about to set sail and Cyrus perked up. From all the hubbub he learned that the ship was called the *Primrose*, and she was bound for a new land far across the sea. The passengers were all poor people who were going there to seek their fortunes.

As the ship moved away from the pier and the crowd called out their last farewells, the booming voice of an old man split the air.

"You're in for trouble!" he bellowed. "You'll never make it! You'll run into the doldrums and be stranded forever! Or a storm will take you under! And if a storm doesn't get you the pirates will! You'll never make it, I say!"

"The old scoundrel," muttered Cyrus. "How could he be so mean as to put a curse on a ship at the start of a voyage!"

The old man had spoiled his fun. Cyrus forgot all about wrecking a ship. Now he was worried about the *Primrose* and all her passengers.

"I'll never know what happens to them," he said, "— not unless I follow. It's a long trip, but then I have nothing better to do." Without making a ripple he ducked under the water to go gliding from the harbor on out to sea, and about a half a mile behind the *Primrose* he came to the surface.

Cyrus could have caught up with the ship in no time, but he didn't want to scare anyone, so he went churning along at a slow, steady pace, careful to keep at a distance.

The first day out all went well. With a lively breeze behind her
the *Primrose* sailed merrily along over a rippling sea without a cloud
in the sky and on into the night with a bright full moon to light
the way.

"So far so good," said Cyrus. "No storms, no pirates and no
doldrums, whatever they are."

For three days the ship sailed along without the least bit of trouble. Then on the fourth day just before sunset a great stillness settled over the sea. There wasn't a breath of breeze, the sails of the *Primrose* fell limp and all at once she came to a stop.

"Well I'll be hornswoggled," growled the captain. "We've run into the doldrums. We've hit a dead calm."

"What'll we do?" someone cried.

"Wait her out and hope for a favoring wind."

"How long will it be?"

"No telling," said the captain. "Maybe a day. Maybe a week or even a month."

"In a month we'd run out of food and water!"

"That we would," said the captain, "but right now we might as well get some sleep."

Cyrus was not a bit sleepy so he stayed up that night circling around the stranded ship trying to figure out some way to help. At last he got an idea.

"Of course," he exclaimed, "how very simple! Very simple indeed!"
Quietly he slipped up close behind the *Primrose*, then very gently
began puffing at the sails and slowly the ship started to move. Soon
she was sailing along over the shimmering sea in a smooth, easy
glide.

He kept the ship going all through the night and then in the rosy
pink hours of the dawn a stiff head wind caught the sails, rocking
the *Primrose* back on her keel.

In an instant the crew and the passengers were on deck with
everyone shouting, "We're out of the doldrums! We're out of the
doldrums!"

"Hold on!" cried the captain. "We're out of the doldrums and heading smack into a squall!"

Black clouds came tumbling over the horizon, there was a great rumble of thunder, and a howling wind was churning up the sea.

"All passengers below!" ordered the captain. Then to his crew he roared, "Reef the top sails! Haul in the mizzen! Tie down the jib! Make her fast, lads!"

In three shakes and a jiffy the sailors were up the rigging pulling in the sails, tightening up the bowlines and mainstays.

And in half a shake the captain and crew popped down the hatch just as a giant wave crashed over the bow. A second wave swept over the deck and the *Primrose* was rocking and reeling. The waves kept coming — great, towering waves — and the ship began to founder.

Cyrus saw in a second that the ship could never last out the storm and he came leaping over the waves to the rescue. He reached the *Primrose* just as she was heeling over and about to go down.

In one desperate lunge he flung his great serpent body around
her hull and then, gulping in air, he puffed himself up into a huge
life preserver. Now Cyrus was unsinkable and with a tight grip on
the ship he carried her high over the crest of the waves.

This way he managed to keep the *Primrose* afloat until the storm finally let up, the wind died down to a whisper and the sea had calmed down to a ripple. Once more shouts of joy echoed from the deck of the *Primrose*. "It was a miracle!" cried the captain. "A bloomin' miracle! I thought sure we were goners!"

"So did I," sighed the serpent as he watched the ship sail away. Cyrus was much too weary and bedraggled to go on, so he flopped down on the sea for a nap and was soon rocked to sleep by the gently rolling waves.

When the sea serpent awakened the *Primrose* was nowhere to be seen.

"Oh well," he said, "I might as well forget about the ship. After all, I've done my bit... But then, she still has a long way to go, and there could be plenty of trouble ahead. All kinds of trouble!"

And away went Cyrus, charging full tilt over the sea to the west.
He searched the sea for miles and miles to find nothing more than
a pelican, and he was about to give up when he sighted a ship on
the horizon.

As he came closer he discovered that *this* ship was flying a black flag. She was a pirate ship! On ahead he spied the *Primrose*. The pirates were chasing her and closing in fast!

"Avast! You lubbers!" roared the pirate captain. "Heave to! Or we'll blast your tub to splinters!"

"The devil take you!" the captain of the *Primrose* roared back. And he kept his ship going full sail.

But there was no hope of outrunning the pirates and in less than a minute they had caught up and pulled alongside.

Then to the sea serpent's horror the pirates opened fire. Twenty cannons exploded with a thundering *BOOM*, blasting the masts of the *Primrose* to splinters! The sails were blown to shreds, and the yard arms came tumbling down.

"The scurvy sea dogs," snarled the serpent. "I'll fix the rascals! I'll shiver their timbers I will!"

Quick as a flash he dove deep into the sea, then wheeling sharply
he shot straight up like a rocket, straight for the pirate ship.

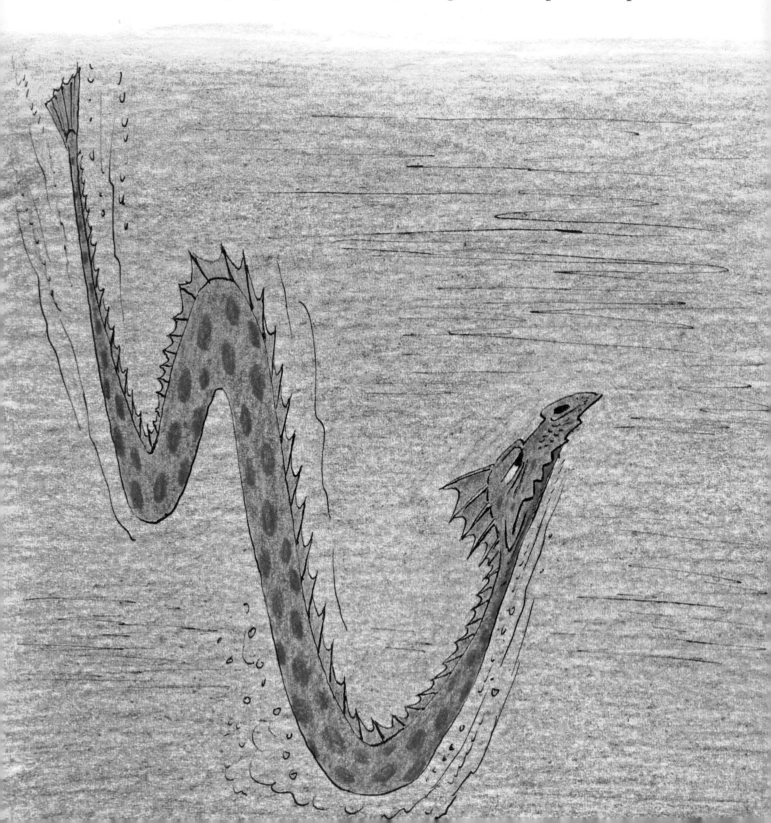

The serpent's hard head caught the ship square in the hull —*KER-WHAM!!!* — and she cracked apart like a nutshell.

The ship was wrecked and so was Cyrus. He had knocked himself out. His eyes were spinning like pinwheels and he sank below the waves as limp as an old shoestring.

When he finally recovered and came to the surface, he was amazed
to find nothing left of the pirate ship but bits and pieces.

The pirates had scrambled aboard a fragment of the hull, dazed
and bewildered, wondering what in the world had hit them.

The crippled *Primrose* was drifting away to the south with the passengers and crew crowded together on the deck. The captain and his crew had seen the giant sea monster destroy the pirate ship with one mighty blow, and they feared their ship would be next.

"If the monster doesn't get us," muttered the captain, "we're done for anyway. There's still a whale of a long way to go and we can't move without sails.

"That old man was right, the one who made such a noise the day we left port. He predicted the voyage would end in disaster. Remember?"

"Who could forget him?" Cyrus muttered to himself. "He was right about the doldrums, the storm and the pirates. But he didn't figure on me. I just might prove him wrong."

The serpent had slipped quietly up to the prow of the ship and was eyeing the anchor chain.

Gripping the chain tightly in his jaws he gave it a tug. He kept pulling until it was strung out to its full length, and all at once the ship lurched forward, bringing cries of terror from the people on board.

"It's the monster!! The sea monster! He's stealing the anchor! No! No! He's pulling us! He's hauling us off to his cave! He'll eat us alive!"

"Hold it!" roared the captain. "How do we know but what he means to help? After all, if he hadn't wrecked the pirate ship the devils would have slit our gullets. And look! He's takin' us west! If he keeps goin' we'll hit land. So let's all cool down and enjoy the ride."

Like a high-stepping steed hitched to a fancy carriage Cyrus galloped over the sea, picking up speed as he went. Never had a sailing ship traveled at such a fast clip.

The serpent was anxious to get the trip over with and he kept the *Primrose* going full tilt night and day without a letup. Finally one morning the lookout was shouting, "Land ho! Land ho!" and sure enough looming over the horizon was a great stretch of land.

At last the perilous voyage was over. With one last burst of speed Cyrus carried the *Primrose* up on the beach, leaving her high and dry. Then with an enormous sigh of relief he headed back out to sea. As he swam on his way the captain and his crew and all the passengers were gathered on a huge rock, and they gave their sea serpent hero a rousing cheer.

"Being a hero is exciting," said Cyrus, "but I've had enough excitement to last for a while. What I need is a good long rest."

Heading south, the giant serpent wandered off into the Caribbean Sea where he found a peaceful little island, and he settled down in the palm trees to sleep for a whole month. Cyrus was very tired for some reason or other.